Pleasure

A Cosmic Current of Spirit

by Billy Scudder

An Ion Drive Publication

Library of Congress

978-0-615-77613-2

Copyright © Billy Scudder, 2012

First Edition; July, 2012

Ion Drive Publishing

IonDrivePublishing.com

Graphics concepts by Billy Scudder

Editing, picture alterations, graphic design, tree- and faerie-hiding
by Rain Livengood.

Additional editing by R. Merlin

Cover photo by Kyer Wiltshire

All the answers you seek

are just behind the veil of forgetfulness...

Contents

Forward,
by R. Merlin

Salami del Amore's 1981 production, with (from left to right) Billy Barrett as Capitano, Q as Pantalone, Dedra Scudder as Isabella, Sandey Grinn as Lelio, Judy Cory as Parmesana and Billy as Arlecchino...

> *"We are the sensory experience of the Creator".*
> -- Billy Scudder

Greetings to Thee, O Gentle Reader,

What you hold in your hands is more than a book; it is the essence of a rare and wondrous human; my friend and comrade, Billy Scudder.

These are things that Billy Scudder believes in: Boundless

Mirth, the power of Joy, the healing rays of the Sun and Moon, the Fae, the Spirit of the Woodland, the untrammeled spirits of children, and an excellent cup of coffee every day at four of the clock.

He is a most inventive and elven and sprightly fellow, given to jollity and warmth and smiles and the Saying of Wise Things. And truly, he is one of the most delightful, imaginative, heartful, magical, and inspiring folk i have encountered in this life.

I first heard about Billy when I started working at the Southern Renaissance Pleasure Faire in Southern California in '82. The Faire was then at the pinnacle of its magicality, and Billy, as the Green Man, carried the Spirit of the Faire and of Springtime along with him as he strolled through the massive throngs, greeted them from the branches of Mighty Oaks, and from time to time surprised them by leaping from the shrubbery.

Billy has played the Green Man for over thirty-five years, ever more perfectly growing into the Spirit of Springtime. His great love for the Natural World has only increased over that time, and has made it ever-easier for him to impart that love unto others. It is our good fortune that he still continues to visit the Faire in his Green Man persona, a widely appreciated living link to the halcyon days of the original Renaissance Pleasure Faire and all those fine old memories...

At that time (as well as today), Billy was a Lot God; one of those folk who was revered and renowned as a Most Excellent Player. Since he had, even at that early time, achieved almost-mythological status, i never expected to actually have the good fortune to have him as a friend and teacher.

And so it wasn't until the '90's that our paths began to cross in various ways. I was surprised to discover that he was actually approachable, and quite agreeable, even willing to listen. I soon learned that he had a lot of wisdom in areas that i lacked; he had raised three daughters, had remained happily with his wonderful wife, Pam, since they had met in 1960 and had dealt with various kinds of adversity, and most importantly, knew what it was that made audiences happy – the skill that i most desired to obtain whilst working at the Faire. I soon resolved that if he felt like talking and needed an audience, i would be it.

Being the Aquarian that he is, he has the gift of clear communication. And also because he is an Aquarian of the first order, his discourses are built upon delightfully spiritual foundations. As a teacher, he has led me to numerous and profound new levels of understanding about myself and the world.

It is my hope that you, gentle reader, will now have similar experiences at his hand, as you come to know this wonderful being through his prose, his poetry, and his ideas about life. Through the pages of this book, he will relate to you stories and poesy inspired by his friends *(Elin's Cakes, Jackamo)*, the passing of his dear sister *(Veleta's Eulogy)*, as well as his takes on the seasons, childhood, the realms of the Fae, what it means to be the Green Man, life and love, and the general structure of Everything.

Over our long association, the following are some of the things that I have learned about Billy: he's an excellent mime, and started at the Faire as one, working with Kathleen Wells and Robert Shields as *Cripplegate Mimes*; he's played Charlie Chaplin for decades, and was the PC Tramp for IBM's first personal computer commercials; he can really sing – at one point, his ambition was to be a crooner; he's good with power tools and can build things (rare for Aquarians); his memory is astonishing – he can remember being born, and what it was like *before* he was born...

He also has a great affinity for Arlecchino, the archetypal trickster in the world of *Commedia del Arte*, and has played this character on numerous occasions with his troupe, Salami del Amore (The Salami of Love), most notably in their production of *Boomba Boomba* in the mid-eighties at Faire, with Sandey Grinn as Lelio, Jack Tate as Scaremello, Mark Lewis as Capitano, Q as Pantalone, and Nancy Heard as Belladona. The cast also included Billy's three daughters, with Dedra as Isabella, Shawn as Barbarella, and Taryn as Mozzerella. At one point in the show, Billy would jump from a first-story platform down onto the stage and do a forward roll into a standing position, all to ecstatic applause; he is also an accomplished actor and has appeared in many films and TV shows, including *Grinch*, where he was Temperature Who of Whoville...

A perfect choice, as Billy has a warm and resonant understanding of the ethos of Christmas; once as I was about to play Santa Clause for the first time he explained it to me thus; "The only thing you have to remember is, Santa is Love."

His joy in the Christmas season is well founded: children are especially drawn to him, sensing an extraordinarily happy/friendly/ amusing new friend, and moreover, a child-like kindred soul. For even though he has faced all the vicissitudes that life can throw at us, he has courageously remained a child-at-heart.

I could go on at great length – oh wait, i already have.

I bid you now go forth and frolic in the fields of his verbiage. Much delight awaits you, and i wish you happy reveling; or, as Billy would say, YIPPEEE!

R. Merlin,
7 July, 2012

Every thing that Is,
is a result of
Nothing's Awareness.

Life only begins
when it becomes aware
that it is Something,
and that it was Nothing.

For out of Nothing

Comes

Everything.

May 1970, Main Stage noon show, Paramount Ranch

Pleasure

Once upon a time, in the midst of social chaos, there was born a moment of Pleasure. It sprang from the hearts of a generation called Love.

It leapt, danced, and sang all the songs of Spring that had lain dormant for hundreds of years.

Like the Phoenix resurrected from its own ashes this Pleasure spread itself over the land and filled the air with sweet music.

The Mother's face watched over all from atop the highest hill, while the Father paraded his radiant smile from morning till night.

In the evening when darkness filled the sky there appeared overhead the dancing of stars, and the Lady Diana protected one and all:

This Pleasure appeared only when winter did wane
Then all would make ready, to Chipping they came
Their trades and their crafts and their laughter they'd ferry
Here under the Oaks all would make merry.

And when we remember all that's gone by
We stop to surrender to each lullaby
Some left for distances unknown and untried
And some souls, we sowed on these hills to abide.
So, while we dreamed, this song of time flew
To all of infinity and back again, new.

And through all this time we protected this Pleasure
Thumbing our noses at those who came closest
To ending our home, and taking our treasure.

But sadly, a feeling so deadly came creeping
It wooed and seduced us to sleep by its side.
It fooled us and told us this sorrow was fleeting
But Pleasure knew better and saw that it lied.

And so to sleep this Pleasure went
While no one knew or attended it
They only knew an emptiness
They filled with outside brews
The dance and song and trade they made
Were paid with heavy dues
Everyone accused each other for things they knew not of
And while they sat in disarray this Pleasure cried above.
"Do not forsake what brought us 'round
Or let it fall from off this ground."

So we ask of everyone, a plea
Break open your hearts, your feelings set free.
Don't harbor your sadness; its up to us all
Gather your strength and answer this call.
Don't stand in the background and cry out in fear
Where is our village that proudly stood here?
Where is the laughter that danced through our tears?
Where are the Oaks that have grown here for years?

If it's sorrow you feel that I've laid all around
Then know how you'll feel if this Pleasure falls down.
They'll hack it, and drag it and blow it around
They'll bash it and mash it, 'til Nothing is found.

Except in the Hearts of all the good folks
Who came here to Chipping Under the Oaks.

The faire is in menopause,
that's why it's lost its period...

The Alchemy of Pleasure

By Ari Berk

Pleasure
is the early morning walk up the hill
and into wonder.

I remember the Faire...
I was five when my parents wandered
with me there,
under the oaks as pennants blew,
snapping in the open air,
and peasants called out their wares
and jewel-toned nobles danced upon carpets,
and I thought: I would live here if could.

I remember
How they put some coins in my hand
and I gave them over to a magus
covered in a leather apron.
A cauldron of lead beside him
was set to bubbling above the coals.
He took my hand in his and guided it to
a ladle of iron.
We lowered it down into the molten soup
and spooned some up.

We held the ladle,
full of swirling silver,
over the water then,
and poured the flowing metal
slowly into a wide wooden bucket.
How the steam
flew up in hissing puffs
and my heart beat fast
as I reached
down
until I was
wet to the shoulder,
down
to the bottom
where the warm,
water-shaped ingot lay.
I clutched that thing,
a memory frozen in time,
a glyph of heat and flame
now past,
and I was spell-stopped
as I drew out a wand
of blended elements,
made by magic,
and the alchemy of Pleasure.

Procession Hill

More Pleasure

I whisper into the stillness that is forever,
and watch as a million images fly by,
of laughing, colorful, and Loving Friends,
who pass in a Parade of Spring time revels,
who all acknowledge a oneness, that only WE who lived
in Chipping Under Oakwood will know.

Take a moment and close your eyes;
remember— the smell of the sage, the mustard, the oak pollen,
Churros, Steak on a Stake, turkey legs, and dark coffee.

See the meadows, with their green and yellow seas of mustard,
dancing with gentle breezes.
Over head, a tapestry of moving burlap canopies unfurl their
rainbow patterns, to the delight of Hawks, Eagles, Sparrows,
and a once-seen Condor.

Where Magic carpets will guide you to The Mullah's dinner table;
where witches, wizards and even some Giants will walk in the
noonday sun...

Where everyone cheered for noontime dancing and singing;
where everyone gathered around a large iron dragon and beat
out tribal rhythms that caused all to jump, dance, and sweat
in the heat of the afternoon sun.
Where the only bath on Saturday night was a Pig.

I still see all that we lived and loved:
Nothing will, or ever will be, what was...

But that place is still alive within me,
and will travel with me always.

If you walked those dusty pathways, and sat under those
majestic Oaks and dreamed yourself into our little village,
tell us what you dreamed...

Childhood

Jumping

　Running

　　Hopping

　　　Skipping

　　　　Scattering

　　　　　Disappearing

　　　　　　Peek-a-booing

　　　　　　　Laughing

　　　　　　　　　Crying

　　　　Jumping

　　　Running

　　Hopping

　　　Skipping

　　Scattering

　　Disappearing

　Peek-a-Booing

Laughing

Crying

Childhood: Don't leave life without one!

Elin's Cakes

Elin was the world's greatest cake maker; and one morning when she was feeling especially happy to be at her work, she heard the front door bell ring. The door opened and then closed with a loud clang: "Just a moment," Elin sang out. She finished the cake she was working on and slipped it into the big cake oven. She was dusting off her hands as she walked into the front of the store. Standing in the middle of the store was a very elegant lady and a small boy. The lady looked and smelled as if she had just stepped out of a catalogue. The little boy was squeaky clean and neat.

Elin asked if she could be of help when the lady interrupted. In a voice that sounded like chalk on a chalkboard she began to describe what she wanted: "I want a Birthday Cake. I want only the very best. It must be rich, thick and creamy... I want it to be chocolate... no, vanilla... no, maybe strawberry. Well, I know it should have purple icing... no, maybe green. Maybe both. I want..."

Elin listened very attentively and watched as the lady described exactly what she wanted the cake to look like. As the lady went on and on, Elin leaned over to the little boy and quietly asked, "What is your name?"

The little boy looked up in surprise, "Who, me?" he said.

"Yes." said Elin.

"My name is Justin Daniels." he replied.

"Is this cake for you, Justin?"

"Yes it is," he said.

"What kind of cake do you think it should be?"

Justin looked at his mother, who was still going on about what a proper birthday cake should be. Justin looked back at Elin and with a very confused look on his face, replied, "I don't know."

Elin smiled at the boy and said, "I have something that will help you think." She reached down with her finger, which was still covered in flour and touched the end of Justin's nose. Justin was surprised and tried to look at the tip of his nose.

"I feel silly," he said. His eyes crossed and blurred, then he began to laugh.

"Silly" said Elin, "like a clown."

"Yes," said Justin, "like a clown in the circus."

Elin's eyes lit up. "Of course, now I have it." She said.

Elin looked over at Justin's mother, "Thank you Ms. Daniels I think I know exactly what you want.

"Well thank you, thank you very much. Please have the cake delivered to my home on Saturday at two o'clock. Here is the address." Ms. Daniels took Justin by the hand, whirled him around, and pulled him out the door just as he was about to say goodbye. All the time she was telling him how much she still had to do to get ready for his party. Elin waved goodbye and returned to her baking, singing a happy tune.

On Saturday morning Elin arrived at the bakery nice and early to make Justin's birthday cake. She took out an old record of circus music. "First I need to set the right mood."

She put the record on her little phonograph and as it began to play, Elin danced over to the worktable. She picked up a wooden spoon and turned to face the phonograph. She began to conduct the music with her spoon. In a cloud of flour and other ingredients the cake began to take shape, and she filled the cake pan and popped it into her big cake oven. After the cake was cool, Elin placed it on a beautiful cake stand. She began to decorate it. She fashioned the sides of the cake to look like a circus wagon then stepped back to think for a moment. "Oh yes, of course," she said. She reached for her special paintbrushes and began to draw a clown face on the top of the cake. First she drew the outline of the clown's head and curly hair. Then she began to draw his face; the nose, one eye and then the other. Elin stopped to look at her work: as she did, the clown's eyes popped open. They began to dance around looking at everything in the bakery and then they looked right at Elin. "Whoopee!" cried Elin, "That is perfect."

Elin began putting the finishing touches on the clown's nose. As she did, the clown looked down to see what she was doing. His eyes crossed, making a very funny sight. Elin reached out and touched his nose with her finger. It made a sound like an old- fashion car horn, *A-Wooo-Ga!* Delighted, Elin began to draw his mouth: it was a big happy smile. She stood back and looked at her creation: the clown was now complete. The clown looked at Elin and made several funny expressions, testing out his new face to see how it felt. Happily, the clown shouted out, "Perfect."

"Oh no, wait," said Elin, "not yet." She picked up the cake and put it into a big cake box. She carried it outside and loaded it into her little delivery truck.

Then Elin went back inside and gathered up all the

necessary supplies for the birthday party: horns, party hats, balloons, and the like. She took them out to her little truck and loaded them in right next to the cake. She closed the door to her little bakery, got into her truck and drove off, once again singing a happy tune.

Elin drove and drove up a mountain road in her little truck with the birthday cake. Higher and higher they went until they were so high that they were above the clouds. At the top of the mountain stood a grand house surrounded by a high fence. In the middle of the fence there was a large open iron gate. She drove through the gate and on up to the front of the big house.

Elin climbed out of her little truck and began unloading all the party supplies and the beautiful cake. She put everything on a special little cart she had just for parties. When everything was loaded she wheeled her little cart to the front door and rang the bell. Inside the house she heard a loud bong. The butler opened the door for Elin. Ms. Daniels, wearing a fancy bathrobe, was standing in the front hall waiting for her. "Oh good, you are on time" said Ms. Daniels. "Right this way; the party is in the back yard."

When they reached the yard, Ms. Daniels called out, "Justin, Justin dear, your Birthday Cake is here. Elin looked around the yard: she saw a long table elegantly set for over a hundred people. Only one person was sitting at the table, Justin.

"What time will the guests arrive?" asked Elin.

"Oh, there will not be any other guests," said Ms Daniels. "There is just too much sickness going around and I didn't want Justin exposed. It will be much safer for him this way with just you and the cake. Well, have a good time, dear," she called over her shoulder, "I'm off to have my nails done for a very important dinner engagement this evening."

Elin turned to Justin and said, "Hello, are you looking forward to your party?"

"Not really," said Justin sadly.

Elin smiled, "Just wait; this is going to be a wonderful party, I promise."

Elin set up her little phonograph. Then she placed the large cake box on the table right in front of Justin. She took out the party hats and favors. She gave a hat to Justin and put one on herself. She started the circus music, went over to the table and sat down next to Justin, "Now we are ready for your party."

"Yes, now we're ready," said Justin, smiling.

Elin stood up and called out in a clear voice, "Ladies and Gentlemen, presenting Justin Daniels' Birthday Cake." The lid of the cake box flew open and a big red balloon rushed out and up into the air. Surprised, Justin looked at Elin and then back at the box just in time to see another balloon rise up from the box and another and another until soon there were balloons of all colors floating in the air above the yard.

As Justin watched, a gloved hand reach up from the box and took hold of one of one of the sides, then another hand reached up and grasped the other side of the cake box. Now Justin could see the top of the clown's head as it began rising up from the box, then his eyes and his big red nose. The clown looked right at Justin and winked. The clown climbed out of the box and jumped down onto the lawn.

Soon he was followed by another clown and then another.

Next, a lovely ballerina and her prancing white horse leaped from the box. Next was a stilt walker and then a funny dancing bear. Soon the whole yard was filled with animals and people with all the sounds and smells of a circus. Justin ran from one wonderful thing to another. He was having the best time of his life.

A window opened on the second story of the big house and his mother called down, "Are you having a good time, dear?" From where Ms. Daniels was seated at her dressing table she could not see the wonderful party.

Justin called back, "This is the best party ever! Thank you, mother."

"You're welcome, dear," she called as she reached over to close the window.

Down in the yard the party continued, Justin was having a fantastic time. He sang and danced and laughed with everyone.

As the afternoon wore on, Justin began to get very sleepy. He sat down at the table to watch the dancing bear, but soon he was fast asleep.

Quietly, Elin guided the clowns, the ballerina and her horse, the stilt walkers, the funny dancing bear and all the other circus animals, back into the big cake box. They all waved goodbye and wished Justin a "Happy Birthday". Just as Elin closed the lid of the box, Justin's mother came out of the house into the yard. She smiled, as she looked over at Justin with his head on the table fast asleep. Elin loaded up her little cart and pushed it back out to her little delivery truck parked in the driveway.

Ms. Daniels picked Justin up and carried him into the big house, up the stairs and into his bedroom. As she was tucking him in his eyes sprang open and in a sleepy voice said, "Thank you, Mommy, for the best birthday party I ever had. I loved the man on the tall stilts and the beautiful ballerina with her prancing white horse and the funny dancing bear, but most of all the clown."

"What clown?' his mother said.

Just then Elin appeared at the bedroom door. "This clown," she said as she held up a big clown doll just like the one on Justin's cake.

"Yes, that clown," said Justin as he pointed to Elin and the doll. Elin walked over to Justin and handed him the doll. "Mommy, can he take a nap with me?"

Ms. Daniels smiled and said, "Of course, dear."

"I love you Mommy, thank you for a wonderful birthday. Thank you for my birthday cake, Elin, and for my clown. I love you, too." Justin closed his eyes hugged his clown doll and sleepily said, "Goodnight."

Elin smiled down at Justin and said, "Goodnight, Justin, and Happy Birthday."

Outside, Elin climbed into her little truck and drove away, singing a happy tune.

1997

Live your legend™

Faerieworlds™

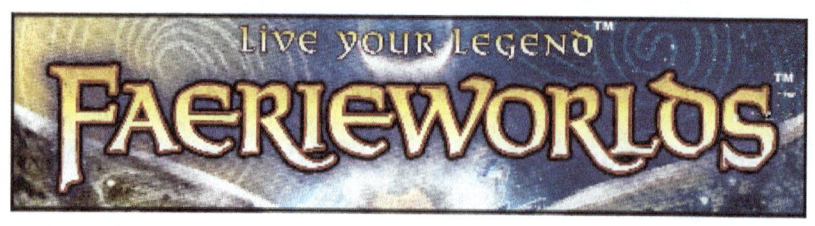

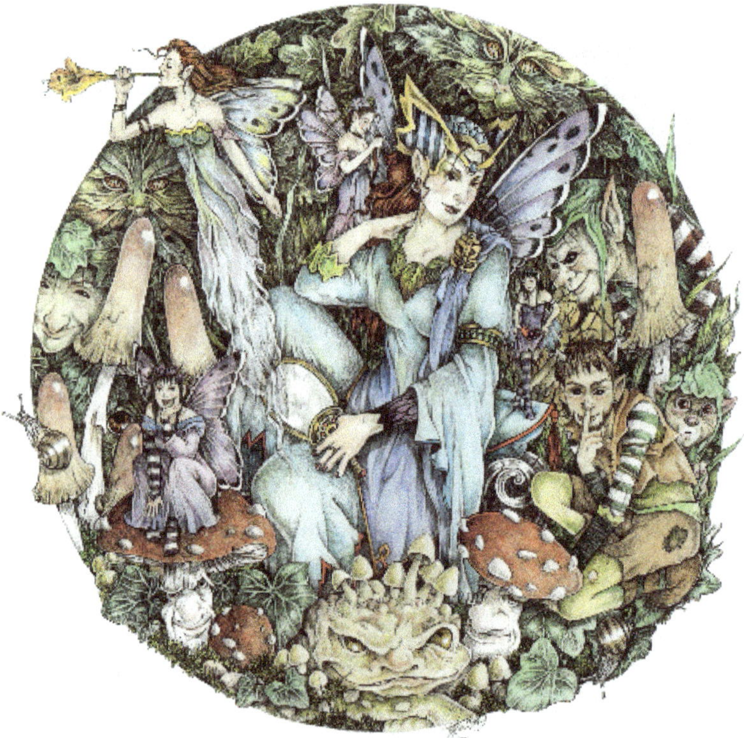

Faerieworlds 2011, the Presence of a Dream

Look around, at all the creative people
   who have come here to be a part of
   what we all acknowledge as *the presence of a Dream*

Have we all Dreamed this into reality?
Or has reality Dreamed us into this collective Fantasy?

Live your life like you're Dreaming

And as you Dream,
   notice how that affects the world around you

As you stand here in your Faerie identity,
   feel how it guides you to a place of knowing,
   and safety.

Close your eyes,
Take a deep breath and let out all the doubt,
Take one more deep breath of Faerie Love,
Keep the Love and let everything else go.
You can feel this any time, by being what you are.
Now open your eyes to your vision of Faerie Love

Use the Magic of the Fae
   as you walk your Life's path

When your travels take you away,
   and the swirling Chaos of the unknown surrounds you,
Stop. Close your eyes, and be what you are now.
Remember...

   "Row, Row, Row your boat gently down the stream,
   Merrily, Merrily, Merrily, Merrily,
   Life is but a DREAM."

   "A dream is a wish your heart makes
      when you're fast asleep.
   In dreams you lose your heartaches,
      whatever you wish for, you keep.
   Have faith in your dreams and someday
      your rainbow will come smiling thru
   No matter how your heart is grieving
      if you keep on believing,
      the dream that you wish will come true."

The presence of a Dream...

We are just the ingredients
that fate molds into history...

Once Before Time

One day Creator called Lobo the wolf, chief of the four-leggeds, to a council. Creator told Lobo he wanted to choose a member of his clan for a very important task. This clan member must be Courageous, Loyal, and Honorable.

"Find the member of your tribe with those qualities and return with them on the next full Moon," said Creator. Lobo agreed, and left for his village. When he arrived at his camp he called all the members of his tribe together for a council. He told them of the Creator's request, and asked everyone to help find the chosen one.

Everyone in the village was excited that one of their own was going to perform a special medicine for Creator.

The next morning, the Sun rose out of the east, spreading Sunlight through all the trees, making them glow gold and green. One single beam of light went right down inside the den and fell upon the sleeping face of a young female wolf-cub.

Lobo was standing outside looking into the den when he saw her face; he could not take his eyes off her face. He called to her and she ran out of the den, with all the other cubs following her. Lobo announced that this day was the first day of Spring, and it was time for some of the cubs to move up the ladder and become full members of the pack.

They would also be given new names. Lobo asked her to come forward, and the cub approached Lobo with her head down.

Lobo said, "Look at me." She lifted her eyes and looked into his, and he said, "From now on, your name is *Morning Light*."

Suddenly a scout came running into the camp, shouting "The Buffalo are coming." Everyone started to dance and sing and run in circles. Lobo started organizing everyone for the hunt. Lobo called Morning Light to his side and told her this was not her day to hunt, that instead she would stay in camp and protect the cubs. Morning Light lowered her head and accepted Lobo's decision.

The pack all gathered together and waited for Lobo's call. He walked back and forth in front of them, looking into their eyes to be sure he had their attention. All of a sudden, he whirled around and gave the call and the pack all followed him quietly out of the camp: the hunt was on!

Courage

All of the younger cubs who were not part of the hunt were very excited, but Morning Light spoke softly and kept circling them, singing a song of calmness. Before long all the young cubs started yawning, and one by one slowly went back into the den and fell asleep. Morning Light then went to the top of the hill above the entrance of the den where she could see the whole village. She lay down, and in the distance she could see the rest of the pack beginning the hunt.

The warm afternoon Sun felt good on her coat. She started to become sleepy so she closed her eyes, but kept her ears up and alert to any sounds. She could hear the hunt and the chase, and in her mind she was part of the pack.

Suddenly, she heard a sound in the camp she'd never heard before: she opened her eyes, and standing right in the middle of the camp was a Wolverine.

He was snorting and sniffing, trying to find the den. She watched quietly as the wolverine found the opening of the den – it was directly under where she was laying. The wolverine was thinking only of his hunger, and started to crawl into the opening. Just as his front legs and head entered the den, she jumped from her perch above the den, landing on his back and knocking him to the ground, which forced all of the air from his lungs. She then grabbed his back leg and started pulling him out of the den.

The wolverine gasped for air and began to fight off his attacker. Then he turned and charged at Morning Light, but she dodged his attack and ran from the camp, away from the den. She led him on a trail that she knew very well, and though the wolverine was chasing her as fast as he could, she ran faster.

She was leading him to a tree that had fallen across a deep ravine. She ran across to the other side, then turned around and came back toward her pursuer. The wolverine was about half way across when she met him, then they snarled and snapped at each other. The wolverine bit onto her nose – so she shook her head, which caused the wolverine to lose his footing, and he slid off the side of the log and fell into the ravine.

She went back to the camp just as everyone was returning from the hunt. When Lobo noticed that she was bleeding and asked her what had happened, she told him about her fight with the wolverine. Lobo told everyone of her courage, and they all sang praises for her brave deed.

Loyalty

One day Morning Light and her best friend and sister, JuJu, decided to go on an adventure. They ran at full speed into the forest, jumping, hiding, and investigating everything in sight. They chased a chipmunk, who cleverly ran behind a tree. They ran from opposite sides thinking they would catch it, but it ran up the backside of the tree. They ran into each other and fell down laughing at their folly; the chipmunk laughed at them also.

All of a sudden, a strong wind blew down from the north and filled their noses with the dark scent of foreboding. A huge black cloud covered the sky, and they began running back to camp. They could hear thunder rolling closer and closer. Lightning started flashing, and rain began to pour down on them. They took shelter under a large tree, but then the lightning struck the top of the tree, causing it to snap in two.

JuJu ran in fear. Morning Light tried to stop her, but her voice was drowned out by the noise of the storm. Then the top of the tree came crashing down on JuJu and swallowed her up under all its branches. Morning Light came running up to where JuJu had disappeared, shouting her name; "JuJu! Where are you?"

Morning Light sniffed and searched for her friend, calling her name. When she crawled under the fallen tree, Morning Light found her. But when she started to pull JuJu out, her friend said, "No, Morning Light! A branch has gone through me." Morning Light started to cry, saying, "No! I can get you out!"

JuJu replied, "No, just stay with me," so Morning Light laid down and started to sing her a lullaby; "Close your eyes, my sweet friend, and rest your weary head. Let go of yesterday's sorrow and let your heart be uplifted by our sweet shared memories: they will always be with me as you will always be with me, and you will always be my beloved sister."

Morning Light sang her this song all night. In the morning the rest of the camp heard her singing and found them. Everyone came, shouting their names. Lobo asked Morning Light what had happened, and she told him how the storm had caught them, and how the rain came, and the lightning, and how it had struck the tree, and how the tree had fallen on JuJu. Lobo said, "We must leave now. Say goodbye to your friend, for now she has gone to live with Creator, in the Land of Forever."

The journey back to camp was very quiet. Lobo let Morning Light walk next to him, so that everyone would know how much he trusted her, and how highly he regarded her loyalty.

Honor

The next day, Lobo called everyone together and announced that the pack was going on a hunt. Everyone leaped and frolicked in their excitement. Lobo told Morning Light that she could join the hunt, but that she should stay in the back of the pack and watch how unselfishly they all worked together. Morning Light was thrilled to be included, and as the pack left the camp she found her place in the back.

A young male was so excited to be in the hunt that he had to follow the pack, but at a distance so no one would see him. Then Lobo led the pack on a path that took them along a cliff above a fast-moving river. The excited cub was not watching where he was walking and slipped off the path, falling down the cliff and stopping just at the river's edge.

Morning Light was at the back of the pack, ahead of the cub, when she stopped, turned her head and looked back down the trail. She sensed something was wrong. She smelled the air deeply and listened intently, seeking the source of her unease.

Morning Light walked back down the trail, then she began to trot, smelling and listening, then she ran. She started feeling fear. As she came to the spot where the cub had fallen, she could hear his cries for help.

When she came to the place where he had gone over, she looked down and saw him, sprawled below at the edge of the river. He got so excited at seeing her that he tried to crawl up the bank, which caused the gravel to slip. As she watched in horror, he slid over the edge of the bank and into the cold river.

As the fast-moving current started carrying him down-stream, Morning Light ran down the path back toward the village, keeping pace with the fast-flowing river and keeping an eye on the cub. When the path came close to the river's edge, she could see that the cub was struggling to just stay above the surface of the water, so she leaped off the path and into the river.

As soon as she entered the water, its coldness surrounded her, but she ignored it and started swimming towards the cub. Morning Light could see that he was not strong enough to fight the current and the cold. Just as he was about to go under, Morning Light grabbed him by the back of his neck and swam towards the shore.

They had been swept down-stream many miles from where they had entered the water. Morning Light pulled the cub up onto the sandy bank, and they both shook the cold water from their coats.

Morning Light found a small trail that led them away from the river and to an open meadow that she did not know. Nothing looked familiar: they were out of their pack's hunting grounds. She knew it would be dark soon, so she began digging a den for the night. When she was done they both crawled in, snuggled up to each other for warmth, and fell asleep for the night.

They awoke the next day to the sounds of their empty stomachs crying out for food. Morning Light started to crawl out of their den just as a ground squirrel came running by the opening. She grabbed it, and they shared their breakfast.

Then they started on their journey home. After several days of walking, they came to a hill that overlooked their village. Morning Light and the cub began to run, and to sing out for all to hear that they had returned to their family.

Everyone greeted them with love and much happiness. The rest of the day was spent celebrating their return with dancing and singing.

The next day, Lobo called everyone together for a council. Lobo said, "We all know who is going to meet Creator."

Everyone shouted, "Morning Light!"

Lobo said, "Yes, you, Morning Light, are the one to

meet Creator. Say your good-byes." After many tears, hugs, and licks, Lobo and Morning Light left the camp. As they walked away the whole tribe sang their love for Morning Light.

Lobo led Morning Light to where he had met Creator. The full Moon was rising as they approached Creator, and Lobo said. "I have a candidate, as you requested."

Creator said to Morning Light, "Come closer." She looked up as Creator looked in her eyes, and then Creator said, "She is perfect."

Lobo asked, "What is the task you want Morning Light to do?"

Creator replied, "Well, you see, the two leggeds have lost their way. They need a teacher to guide them back to what they have forgotten. Morning Light will show them how to once again become loyal, courageous, and honorable."

Creator continued, "And when they have regained these three qualities, they will again be able to accept all of their lost and wandering people back into their tribe, and once more become as One. You, Morning Light, will be their guide and teacher in this.

Creator smiled, and said, "You will forever be my reflection, and you will now live with them, and they will call you DOG."

Did You Feel That?

Did you feel that?

Yes! Was it an Earth Quake?

It was Mother Earth, getting our attention.

We have not been aware of Mother Earth's warning signs

Did you notice how you all held on to each other? In times of peril people gather together and forget what keeps us apart.

Who here is the web of life?

We are not the web of life. We are merely a strand in it.
What we do to the strand we do to the web.

We are all fleas on the back of a great dog.
Stop trying to control or kill the dog.

Mother Earth is a garden.

Our job is to be the gardeners.

Treat your self like a garden, cultivate and plant good things.
Not selfishness and greed.

Take care of your Garden and it will take care of you

Out of the Garden

Violence, in contemporary society, is a result of misdirected survival instincts in humans. Man puts himself outside of the laws of nature. He did that when he (metaphorically) left the Garden and chose the path of intellect. Natural law and the universe unto itself is violent. For example: a supernova is not a humble occurrence in nature. It is a natural act of violence. There is no life form that does not exist without the absorption of another life form.

Everything humans consume as food was once living.

That food source is what nourishes and sustains our lives. The problem is that we have no association with the killing of our food. It is done by someone else, so most people have no identity with the violence committed against their food choices. We somehow instinctively know that this violence exists but because we don't commit the violent act ourselves to get our food, we seek violence vicariously. Until we can accept the responsibility and respect for all forms of life we are destined to live in the darkness of our own ignorance of what life and death are.

1997

The root of all that's Wicked,
is the Knowledge of it...

For Wickedness
cannot exist
in the heart of the Innocence.

Ignorance or Truth

There are no Secrets!
There is only ignorance of the Truth

What is known can never be unknown...

Unless your capacity to know the Truth
outweighs your ability to understand,
your Ego needs to remain ignorant of the Truth!

Oh! To heal that which has pained you for all this time.

Let it out into the light for all to feel.

Let us all regain our pride.

Seek not to cause more pain, from pain that's deep inside.

We must not seek vengeance on other innocent victims
to stop this pain of shame.

All this pain has caused us to separate ourselves as humans.

Once we acknowledge each other as humans we'll stop this pain
of shame.

Empty Faces

Empty faces gazing blindly
Eyes are frightened screaming nightly
Souls on fire cracking lightning
Breaking minds ever lasting
Quench the gnawing rodent's hunger
Rip away the roach's collar
Give me life for one more hour
Bring in secret earth's surrender
I can't breathe without this hunger
Quickly! Screaming gently
Prick my skin and enter smoothly
Shooting life into my head....
Oh! What sweet nova feeling
Brings desire to an ending
My ending now is my beginning.
Bring on death I welcome gladly
How I wish for sunshine's dawning
That will find me tomorrow's brother...

Fear is self-exile from joy...

Speak With The Angels

Listen to the silences of their Sacred voices
Let your heart beat to the rhythm of their heart
You are always in the presence of the Divine

Just be still, Let your breath quiet,
the turmoil you run from,

Accept your pain of loneliness to end;
allow what you choose, not what you Fear,

Come now and Speak With The Angels.

You never have to give up what you believe,
To support someone else's insecurities.

Allow

Never allow your opinion to guide you away from reason.

Never allow your ego, to lead you into serving selfish goals.

Never allow anger to let you unjustly accuse friends by
rationalizing ignorance.

Allow yourself not to know everything.

Allow yourself the freedom to be wrong.

Allow all people to be the altar at which you worship.

Accept your emotional frailties.
Their season will come and go.

As the wheel turns view all things without judgment.

Love is the Answer!

Song of the Green Man

I stand in the present and reflect on my past
adventures and the adventures waiting to become
the gift that is life's unfolding presence.

I pray I have the wisdom to see the truth,
and not the illusions created by fear and ignorance.

I speak to all my life experiences as a guide to help
me understand how my shadow falls across my many
relationships with those who travel in this great
mystery.

I ask all to forgive each other's frailties and just be,
"The Children of Love".

Aglow

Once upon a winter's evening
As the midnight mist glistened on our window pane
There came a tapping at the skylight door
We opened quickly this door of glass
And in there flew a great Aglow

It shimmered and sparkled and danced on its toes
It tickled us silly and filled us with dizzy
It turned upside down inside out over and under
It was but a moment, it could have been longer
No one seems to remember
For in that time of timelessness all things great and small were
joined as one

And as we dared to take it further
It sprang so fast it split the air
With grace beyond compare
And out our door of glass it shot like an arrow to its mark
We watched it steak into the night
And saw it fade out of our sight

We will fondly remember for the rest of our nights
This little light that made us all
Aglow

Jackamo

(This piece was written with the late great Jack Albee in mind).

Open with a montage of circus images, crowd sounds, and circus music. The star of the circus, Jackamo, the world's greatest clown, makes his appearance. He tries to begin his act but is interrupted by a tugging at his coat. He shoos it away and begins again only to be interrupted by the same tugging. Once more he shoos it away without even looking down. We see a small clown standing at his side looking very anxious and concerned. He shifts from foot to foot and tugs again at the great Jackamo's coat tails. Finally, after many tries to brush this irritation away Jackamo looks down at the small clown.

Jackamo: What is it?

The small clown points to his overcoat and opens it and on the inside we see and hear a ringing alarm clock. The ringing gets louder and louder. Jackamo picks him up and starts to shake him.

Cut to:

Jack, sitting up in bed, shakes his alarm clock. His room is small and used-looking with old and drab furniture. There is a circus poster on the wall and an old easel with an unfinished canvas and paints scattered around. This is not "The world's most famous clown;" it is only Jack. It was all a dream. Jack gets out of bed and begins to get ready for work.

Cut to exterior:

Jack comes out of an old apartment building and gets into his paint truck. The truck is covered in paint splashes and the back is full of paint and supplies. Jack is a sign painter. He drives away.

We see Jack setting up his equipment for a day's work. He sets a stool up in front of a large window. There is another large window to his right. He sits down and begins to paint the sign. We see Jack's image painting the sign in the window to the right. He is dabbing paint on his brush from an old paper plate that has seen much use. He looks over and sees his reflection in the window and he begins talking to himself. We follow the movement of the paint brush from pallet to window from Jacks POV. As the brush reaches the window the reflection is now Jackamo the clown from his dream.

Jack: I could have been a great actor.

Jackamo: Or a great clown.

Jack: Shut up. I'm not talking to you.

Jackamo: I know. I'm talking to you.

Jack does a double take at his reflection.

Jack: Listen, I don't have time to argue with you.

Jackamo: You're not.

Jack: What?

Jackamo: How can you argue with yourself?

Jack: Easy, I do it all the time.

Jackamo: Timeless chatter. That's all it is.

He imitates Jack's movements.

Jack: Cut that out. Stop it!

Jackamo: Make me.

Jack: Oh yeah?

Jackamo: Yeah!

Jack makes animal noises and movements. Jackamo does the same. They do a mime mirror exercise. Jack does a big finish and throws his hat to the ground.

A passerby applauds, throws a coin in Jack's hat and walks away.

Jackamo: I told you that you could be a clown. All you need is the make-up.

Jack: I don't have any.

Jackamo: Then paint your face.

We see Jack start to paint his face. He is looking in the window trying to copy Jackamo's face exactly.

From Jackamo's POV we see Jack finish the make-up. He picks up a bag and fashions a hat just like Jackamo's.

Jack: How's this? (He strikes a pose)

From Jack's POV we are looking up at the reflection, and now everything is changed. Instead of Jackamo in the window we see Jack as he was before the make-up.

Jack: What happened?

Jackamo: You released me by creating my reflection outside of the glass and now I am real.

Jack: I don't want to stay in here. I want to come out now.

Jackamo: Sorry Jack. See you later. (He laughs as he walks away).

We see Jack's reflection follow him to the end of the window. A small crowd has gathered. As Jackamo walks toward them they applaud. A large black limo slides up to the curb. A chauffeur gets out and opens the door. Jackamo bows to the crowd gets into the limo and it drives away.

We see a montage of images of Jackamo. He is the world's greatest clown. He's on Letterman, Leno, etc., etc. but each time he passes in front of a mirror or window we see his reflection as Jack trying to get out. Jackamo never looks into the glass.

Cut to ext:

Jackamo is getting out of a Limo at a very regal hotel. The marquee reads, "Tonight, Jackamo The World's Greatest Clown". The manager is falling all over himself trying to gain his favor.

Manager: We have reserved our finest suite for you, Jackamo.

We see them go up in the elevator to the penthouse.

Manager: Please feel free to call me directly if you need anything or if I can be of service to you in any way.

Jackamo: Thank you. I will rest now before the performance tonight. See that I am not disturbed.

The manager backs out of the penthouse and closes the door. Jackamo opens the door to the bedroom and walks in. He looks around, walks to another door, opens it, and goes in. As he does, he turns on the light. We see that he has entered a dressing room. There are mirrors on every wall and on the back of the door. Jackamo looks at his reflection. There is Jack. But now there are four Jacks surrounding him. Jackamo reacts: he tries to escape but

Jack is too quick for him the door closes and he is trapped. There is a big slapstick brawl with the four Jacks. Finally Jack is victorious.

Jack: You must let me back into the world. You must return to the glass.

Jackamo: I will if you promise me one thing.

Jack: What?

Jackamo: Promise first.

Jack: Okay. What do you want?

Jackamo: Once a day for ten minutes you must put on the make-up and be Jackamo, The World's Greatest Clown.

Jack: I agree.

Slowly we see the image of Jackamo fade and in his place we see Jack the sign painter. In the mirrors we see only Jack.

There is a knock at the door. Jack looks up.

Jack: Yes. What is it?

(From behind the door we hear...)

Ten minutes, Jackamo.

Jack smiles at his reflection and begins to apply his make-up.

Music over. The same circus music we heard in the beginning.

What is Forever?

What ever isn't NOW.

The Kiss

Oh, that sacred place;

I seek thy shelter.

Come quickly,

Touching softly but firmly,

Its wetness surrounding

And warmly welcoming me

Into its door...

Oh what sweet tastes fill

This empty space

With gleeful joys...

What cathedral bells

Announce this bliss

With just these lips

When they Kiss

The Problem with the Sexes

The problem with the sexes is nothing more than a chromosomal misinterpretation. You see, women are more women than men are men. A woman gets an X gene from her mother...

And an X gene from her father, which means she is totally what she is. A man gets an X gene from his mother, and a Y gene from his father. Which means he is half X and half Y. That is why men are afraid of women: they're always out-numbered, chromosomally.

So more correctly, men are Wo-man or Fe-male, and girls are Wo-Wos and Fe-Fes.

62

Sorrow is a result of yesterdays' remembered incompletions

Tears are a result of knowing that tomorrow will bring yesterdays' remembered incompletions

Joy is a result of knowing that tomorrow is not yesterday or tomorrow, but just the NOW of Always...

When NOW Becomes

Can you feel it?
As its presence becomes so profound
that your anticipation fills you with
the Joy of its promise.

This moment is upon us.
Welcome it, let it fill your being with
Joyful, Blissful, Acceptance.

When, before we rushed to welcome it,
we had not known what it knew.
But it knew we would remember
what we forgot to know.

Let NOW, be all we know;
Stay in this moment.
We can make this last Always.

Be Now!   Be Now!   Be Now!

As long as you stay within this
place of Sacred space,
time will not erase this feeling of timelessness.

Open all the locked doors to the treasures
you've been keeping deep inside your pain of shame.
Let go of all that's not NOW.

Be Now!   Be Now!   Be Now!

My Brother's Voice

I heard my Brother's voice today,
speaking from across the ages of time.
His Voice sounded like the wind,
gently moving through the trees,
awakening secrets,
that have been sleeping away the seasons.

As he spoke, I witnessed how our ancestral fires
lit up our long houses with wisdom that defies laws,
whose truths grow out of their hearts
like Spring flowers.

Our truths are not their truths, for their truths are
written on pieces of paper that they wave in your face.
Our truths are in our hearts and our words.

Do not speak to me of things that mean nothing,
that are absent of living truth.
Some peoples say they know the truth,
but their words are empty of the voice of The Creator.

Remember we are all children of the great cauldron.
Without Mother Earth and The Great Spirit,
we are just Star dust.

Autumn

Orange and amber danced through my window today
And gleefully rolled and slid across my floor
They warmly brushed against the side of my couch
I breathed deep this warmness
And it filled me from head to toe
The air outside stopped and starred
Then quickly ran in all ways as fast as it would
'Cause it could
The leaves on the trees cheered and wagged
Themselves like tongues
So much so they left their home
These branches where they were born
And flew up high across the sky
This way and that way, every which way
They tried to fly with abandoned pride
When all of a sudden the wind evaporated
Leaving them to fall from their place in the sky
And float gently down upon the ground
There they stayed and melted away
To sleep their night till May

Veleta's Eulogy

Oh Morpheus, come swiftly with your cloak of sleep,
And rescue this weary traveler.

Help guide her to her final destination,.
A path we all must travel one day.

She will live within us, as long as we remember her.

Her spirit is now with the Creator,
And has become part of the forever.

We are here left in the confusion and chaos of what is,
And Veleta is in the calmness of what was.

Our lifes' path is still becoming,
And moving us towards our lifes' goal.

Be ever present on your journey and don't become the
unfortunate, who sleep through the Blessing which is life.

Be Life-like, be Alive, nourish every moment.
Be the gift you want to be in the Present.

Infinity = A hypothetical reference to an incomprehensible place

Sunrise

The Sun rises and spreads its light over the lands and seas. And everything comes into being.

Life itself comes out of the darkness, Of the Great Mother, into the world of possibilities.

Where it begins its journey.

Just as the Sun crosses the sky above us, so does your life travel and carry you through the events that make up your life's experiences.

As the Sun passes noon it starts its journey to rest. As our life passes from morning, to noon, to dusk, we must learn to honor all the phases of our life's Day. And joyfully accept our retreat into sunset.

As the Sun sets and slumber surrounds all things
Remember we lived once for Always

Sunset

Remember:
Don't be the problems in life!
Be the Answer

Be Free

Be free
Feel it
Go ahead, reach for it
It's right in front of you
Grab it
Let it lift you
It can make you flyeeeeeeee!

Soar above the things that hold you still
That's it
Just let go
Yes you can
Open your heart unleash your spirit
Breathe deep the freshness you now feel
Be Freeeeeeeeeeeeeeeeee!

Ari Berk

Ari Berk is the author of *The Secret History of Giants* (NCTE Notable Award winner), *William Shakespeare—His Life and Times* (UK's SLA Children's Choice Award winner), and numerous other books for children and adults including *The Runes of Elfland* (with artist Brian Froud), *The Secret History of Hobgoblins*, *The Secret History of Mermaids*, *Coyote Speaks*, and most recently, *Death Watch* (Book One of *The Undertaken Trilogy*), and *Nightsong* (illustrated by Loren Long). When not writing, he moonlights as a professor of mythology and folklore. He lives in Michigan with his wife and son. Visit him at ariberk.com

Brian Froud

Fiery Faerie, page 48

Blue Faerie, page 62

Brian Froud for over forty years has been regarded as the pre-eminent faerie artist in the world, and an authority on faeries and faerie lore. His international best-selling book, *Faeries* with fantasy and Tolkien illustrator Alan Lee is considered a modern classic. His landmark work with Jim Henson as conceptual designer on feature films *The Dark Crystal* and *Labyrinth* along with other Henson projects- set new standards for design, puppeteering and animatronics in film. These films are considered landmarks in the evolution of modern day special effects and attract an international cult following. With over 8 million books sold to date, Brian's international best sellers include *Lady Cottington's Pressed Fairy Book*, *Good Faeries / Bad Faeries*, *The Faeries' Oracle* and more. His latest books are *The Heart of Faerie Oracle* with Wendy Froud and *How to see Faeries* with John Mathews, both published by Abrams Books.

WorldOfFroud.com

Wendy Froud

Wendy Froud has been a doll maker since the age of five. As soon as she could bend a pipe cleaner and tape bits of fabric together she began to make the kinds of dolls she couldn't buy: dolls of centaurs and satyrs, unicorns and faeries, all to populate her childhood world. She continues to do so to this day. Wendy worked as sculptor and puppet builder for Jim Henson for many years, primarily on the films *The Dark Crystal* and *Labyrinth*. She sculpted "Jen" and "Kira" for *The Dark Crystal*, she also fabricated "Yoda" for *The Empire Strikes Back*. Other work for Jim Henson included *The Muppet Movie* and *The Muppet Show*. Her work has been featured in three books created with fantasy author Terri Winding: *A Midsummer Night's Faerie Tale*, *The Winter Child* and *The Faeries of Spring Cottage*. Her latest book *Heart of Faerie Oracle* is published by Abrams Books.

"The first time I met Billy, he was dressed as the Greenman and he embodied the very spirit of Faerieworlds. Weaving through the crowds , stopping to chirp and tweet at children and adults alike, Billy wove a spell over everyone who gathered there. He never spoke, never broke character and consequently was never quite human but instead a visible element of the faery realm walking among us. And that was how I thought of him – a spirit, a brightness, and a link between the worlds.

"When I finally met Billy out of the guise of the Green Man, I found a man just as magical out of costume as in it. A wise, gentle and deeply spiritual person emerged from behind the mask of Ivy leaves and I saw again a face of Faerie, a face that could look into both worlds and find joy and wisdom in either one."

I met Brian and Wendy Froud the first year I worked for Faerieworlds In Eugene, Oregon. I was so excited to meet them that I brought all of the books and calendars of theirs that I had for them to sign, and they did. Over the years that I have worked with them they have encouraged me to write something – so, about a year ago, I started to find all the scraps of paper with things I had been writing, and started this book. I took our first draft with me to Faeriecon in November 2011 and gave it to them to read. About two hours later they returned it, and told me they both had read it and loved it. Then they asked if I would like some art for the book, at which point I almost started weeping. Wendy said I should ask other artists from Faeriecon to contribute to the book, because I was the face of this community; then I *did* start weeping. I felt such Love from them it was like a warm blanket on a cold night.

The Frouds have a new book coming out in the Autumn of 2012, called "Trolls." It is a collaboration between Wendy and Brian, being a combination of images, stories and troll facts.

WorldOfFroud.com

Jen Delyth

Cover illustration border from *Yggdrasil*

Jen Delyth is a Welsh artist who creates original paintings and illustrations which explore the language of myth and symbol inspired by Celtic Folklore and the Spirit within nature. Her body of work spans an array of media including traditional egg tempera painting, oil painting, printmaking and textile design as well as computer illustrations and multimedia animation.

Limited edition giclees are made by the artist in her studio using archival materials and inks to produce fine art museum quality prints. Jen Delyth's original Celtic artwork has been widely published and exhibited in North America, in her native Wales and throughout Europe. Recent work includes a series of Celtic Animations collaged with Celtic poetry and music available as an interactive DVD titled *Beyond the Ninth Wave*. Jen's new book, *Celtic Folk Soul,* is a retrospective of her artwork and writing inspired by the last 20 years.

We met at Faeriecon the first year in Philadelphia, and every time we speak she reminds me of fresh heather blowing in a gentle breeze. Her understanding of the natural world is always warm and nourishing.

http://celticartstudio.com

Alan Katz

 *The Wit Off,* page 50

I met Alan Katz in 1983. We were with a group of people who formed a guild that we named "The Fools Guild". Most of us worked at the Southern California Renaissance Faire in the 1970s. Most of the members lived in a house in Hollywood. This house was entirely built of Redwood in the 'twenties. It

looked like a church, and was historic- the legend was that Frank Lloyd Wright lived in this house for a while. It was a party House in the 70's and 80's and one of their big parties was The Feast of Fools, held on April 1st, at which Alan started painting all the fools. He and I and several other fools would get together once a week and discuss foolery. One of the other Fools was Jack Albee, who lived his life like a fool; speaking his mind all the time. Alan and I loved Jack, and his views of the world – he came from a family of artists whose works are in museums. Jack also, at different times of the year, would paint store windows in Hollywood. One day I was watching him getting ready to go and paint some windows, and he was talking about himself and clowning, and I thought of this story, *Jackamo*. Alan painted a picture of Jack and the other fools, having a contest to see who was the funniest fool, called *The Wit Off*. I asked Alan if I could use part of his picture for this book.

Elin Katz

Elin's Cakes, page 10

Elin Katz is owner and creator of Rosebud Cakes in Beverly Hills, CA. This shop creates artistic cakes that would be perfect for bringing something truly unique to any celebration. Rosebud is actually a cake design studio, rather than a bakery store. No other cake store offers the range of creativity and commitment to quality- from the visual impact to the exquisite flavor of every cake. Elin trained to be an artist and she proves that with each project she takes on.

The first time I visited her in her new store, she walked out from the kitchen in her baking clothes and baker's hat and there was flour all over her. She looked so beautiful that she inspired me to write *Elin's Cakes*. For more information you can contact her at:

Rosebud Cakes
www.rosebudcakes.com

Helena Nelson-Reed

Flaming Arrow, frontispiece; *The May Queen,* page 8;
The Visitor, page 38; *Springtime,* page 42

Axis Mundi, page 58; *The Flowering,* page 60; *The Unexpected,*
page 66; *Dryad's Farewell,* page 68

Helena Nelson-Reed is an American visionary artist specializing
in luminous watercolor and fine art illustration. Published
works include cover art for magazines and books, along with
imagery portrayed in *The Call of the Goddess* calendars, cards,
Native American Spirit, and *Visions of the Shaman* cards. Her
primary focus is the portrayal of archetypal imagery, exploring
the collective consciousness evident in fairytale, myth, and
shamanism as well as personal dreams and experiences. her
work is often described as emotionally moving and lovingly
created in extraordinary detail, pushing the medium of
watercolor into exciting new areas.

Helena and I met at Faeriecon and I instantly felt as if I had met one of my lost Sisters. Over the last couple of years I realized how much we had in common. When I told her about this book she encouraged me to complete it, and offered to contribute some of her amazing art. I am humbled by her generosity and kindness.

www.helenanelsonreed.com

http://dancingdovestudio.blogspot.com

Linda Ravenscroft

Titania and Puck, page 18; *Autumn's Fall,* page 32; *The Perfect Sphere,* page 34; *The Emergence of Spring,* page 70

Linda Ravenscroft is an internationally acclaimed British fantasy watercolorist. Her delicately detailed and vibrant faeries can be found on jigsaw puzzles, T-shirts, cards, figurines and many other licensed products. In addition, she offers prints and original paintings to her customers through her on-line web gallery. Linda has been painting fantasy imagery since she was a child. She finds it's a way to escape the mundane and sometimes terrible "real world." Her books include *Enchanted: The Faerie and Fantasy Art of Linda Ravenscroft,*

How to Draw and Paint Fairyland, *Fairy Artists Drawing Bible*, and *The Mystic Faerie Tarot* as well as numerous calendars.

I met Linda and John Ravenscroft at Faeriecon in Baltimore and we played a lot. Every time I hear Linda's voice I'm somehow transported back in time to an English country estate where images are so vivid I can recall them for hours. When I told her about my book and asked her to contribute, she gleefully said "Yes". This has inspired me to keep writing.

http://www.lindaravenscroft.com

Thank You

I would like to take a moment to thank several people for this incredible journey of discovery.

When I was young, the world didn't know me – or let me say *I* didn't know me. There were a couple of people who did notice me, however. They encouraged me to be me. They always told me to march to my own drummer, and follow my dreams. One was my neighbor, Joan Thornburg; the other one was Jerry Hoke. They both spent hours talking to me about listening to the unfolding story that is the great mystery of life.

My wife and family also gave me that same confidence. My wife, Pamela, and I have been married for 50 years and throughout that time she was always telling me to write. Even my children were telling me to write.

About a year ago my good friend Merlin told me he could publish a book of mine, so I started emailing him all the scraps of things I had been stashing for years. He kept encouraging me to send everything to him. Last October, Merlin put everything into a book and sent it to me as a sample. As I started to read the first draft I was overwhelmed with emotion.

The artists who have contributed to this book have filled me with such love and encouragement that I will always remember their kindness.

After all the art was collected I started working with Rain Livengood on layout and design; what a master of computer graphics! His creative help on this project was a blessing.

My Brother Merlin and I have been friends for over thirty years. He is one of the most giving, gracious, and inspiring humans I've ever known.

So I say THANK YOU to all who have held my hand and walked with me on this Magical journey.

Billy, July 2012

www.ingramcontent.com/pod-product-compliance
Lightning Source LLC
Chambersburg PA
CBHW070630120726
47909CB00004B/1383